This Book Belongs to...

_____

Library of Congress Cataloging-in-Publication Data
Thomas and the school trip / illustrated by Owain Bell. p. cm.— "Based on the railway series by the Rev. W. Awdry." SUMMARY: Attempting to hurry through his work so that he can give some schoolchildren a ride, Thomas the Tank Engine must overcome a series of obstacles.
[1. Railroads—Trains—Fiction. 2. School field trips—Fiction.] I. Bell, Owain, ill. II. Awdry, W. Railway series. III. Series. PZ7.T3696 1993
[E]—dc20 92-33711 ISBN 0-679-84365-5(trade)

Printed in the United States of America 10 9 8 7 6 5 4 3 2 1

GROLIER
BOOK CLUB EDITION

THOMAS
and the
SCHOOL TRIP

Based on *The Railway Series*
by the Rev. W. Awdry

Illustrated by Owain Bell

BEGINNER BOOKS
A division of Random House, Inc.

It is a big day
in the train yard.
"Let's get ready!"
says Thomas
the Tank Engine.

Swish, swish.

The train yard is ready.

Rub, rub.

Scrub, scrub.

The engines are
bright and shiny.

Blue, green, red.

Thomas, Henry, and
James are ready too.

Even Sir Topham Hatt
is ready.

Ready for what?
Children—
on a school trip!
"Peep! Peep!
Here they come!"
shouts Thomas.

"Hello, hello," he puffs.

"My name is Thomas.

Watch me push!

Watch me pull!"

Thomas has lots of fun.

But soon Thomas
has to go.
He has work to do
on his branch line.

Poor Thomas.

He is sad.

He wants to stay.

He wants to play.

Sir Topham Hatt
has an idea.
"Do your job, Thomas.
Then hurry back.
You can take
the children home.

But remember.

You cannot be late.

You must be on time.

Or somebody else

will take the children."

"I will hurry.
I will hurry,"
Thomas says.
His coaches Annie
and Clarabel say,
"We will hurry too."

Chug, chug, chug.
All along his branch line,
Thomas goes as fast
as he can.

Up a hill.

Over a bridge.

Through a tunnel.

Thomas stops
at every station.

At last!
The work is done.
"Right on time.
Right on time,"
chugs Thomas.

"Now hurry back.
Hurry back,"
puff Annie and Clarabel.

But Thomas
cannot hurry.
Thomas has to wait.

And wait.

And wait again.

Oh no!

Will Thomas be late?

Will James or Henry

take the children home?

Oh my!
Now what is that
up ahead?
It is Bertie the Bus.
He has broken down.

Thomas wants to help.

But then he will be late—

much too late.

Stop or go.

Help or hurry.

What should Thomas do?

Screech!
Thomas stops.
He cannot leave
his friend.

"Will you take
my passengers?"
asks Bertie.

Look!
It is the children!
Bertie was taking
them home.

Hooray for Thomas!

He has saved the day!